THE LOST HOUSE

BY

RICHARD HARDING DAVIS

British Library Cataloguing-in-Publication Data
A catalogue record for this book is available from the
British Library

Contents

Richard Harding Davis

Richard Harding Davis was born on 18th April 1864, in Philadelphia, Pennsylvania. He was the son of two writers, Rebecca Harding Davis (a prominent author), and Lemuel Clarke Davis (a journalist and editor of the Philadelphia Public Ledger).

Davis attended Lehigh University and Johns Hopkins University, but was asked to leave both due to neglecting his studies in favour socialising. With some help from his father, Davis was able to find a position as a journalist at the Philadelphia Record, but was soon fired from the post. He then spent a short time at the Philadelphia Press before moving to the New York Evening Sun, where he became a controversial figure, writing on subjects such as execution, abortion, and suicide. He went on to edit Harper's Weekly and write for the New York Herald, The Times, and Scribner's Magazine.

During the Second Boer War in South Africa, Davis was a leading correspondent of the conflict. He saw the war first-hand from both parties perspectives and documented it in his publication With Both Armies (1900). Later in his career he wrote a story about his experience on a United States Navy ship that shelled Cuba as part of the Battle of Santiago de Cuba. His article made the headlines and prompted the

Navy to refuse to allow reporters aboard their vessels for the remainder of the war.

He wrote widely from locations such as the Caribbean, Central America, and even from the perspective of the Japanese forces during the Russo-Japanese War. He also covered the Salonika Front in the First World War, where he spent a time detained by the Germans on suspicion of being a spy.

Davis married twice, first to Cecil Clark in 1899, and then to Bessie McCoy in 1912, with whom he had one daughter. Davis died following a heart attack on 11th April, 1916, at the age of 51.

I

It was a dull day at the chancellery. His Excellency the American Ambassador was absent in Scotland, unveiling a bust to Bobby Burns, paid for by the numerous lovers of that poet in Pittsburg; the First Secretary was absent at Aldershot, observing a sham battle; the Military Attache was absent at the Crystal Palace, watching a foot-ball match; the Naval Attache was absent at the Duke of Deptford's, shooting pheasants; and at the Embassy, the Second Secretary, having lunched leisurely at the Artz, was now alone, but prepared with his life to protect American interests. Accordingly, on the condition that the story should not be traced back to him, he had just confided a State secret to his young friend, Austin Ford, the London correspondent of the New York REPUBLIC.

"I will cable it," Ford reassured him, "as coming from a Hungarian diplomat, temporarily residing in Bloomsbury, while en route to his post in Patagonia. In that shape, not even your astute chief will suspect its real source. And further from the truth than that I refuse to go."

"What I dropped in to ask," he continued, "is whether the English are going to send over a polo team next summer to try to bring back the cup?"

"I've several other items of interest," suggested the Secretary.

"The week-end parties to which you have been invited," Ford objected, "can wait. Tell me first what chance there is for an international polo match."

"Polo," sententiously began the Second Secretary, who himself was a crackerjack at the game, "is a proposition of ponies! Men can be trained for polo. But polo ponies must be born. Without good ponies——"

James, the page who guarded the outer walls, of the chancellery, appeared in the doorway.

"Please, Sir, a person," he announced, "with a note for the Ambassador, he says it's important."

"Tell him to leave it," said the Secretary. "Polo ponies——"

"Yes, Sir," interrupted the page. "But 'e won't leave it, not unless he keeps the 'arf-crown."

"For Heaven's sake!" protested the Second Secretary, "then let him keep the half-crown. When I say polo ponies, I don't mean——"

James, although alarmed at his own temerity, refused to accept the dismissal. "But, please, Sir," he begged; "I think the 'arf-crown is for the Ambassador."

The astonished diplomat gazed with open eyes.

"You think—WHAT!" he exclaimed.

James, upon the defensive, explained breathlessly.

"Because, Sir," he stammered, "it was INSIDE the note when it was thrown out of the window."

Ford had been sprawling in a soft leather chair in front of the open fire. With the privilege of an old school-fellow and college classmate, he had been jabbing the soft coal with his walking-stick, causing it to burst into tiny flames. His cigarette drooped from his lips, his hat was cocked over one eye; he was a picture of indifference, merging upon boredom. But at the words of the boy his attitude both of mind and body underwent an instant change. It was as though he were an actor, and the words "thrown from the window" were his cue. It was as though he were a dozing fox-terrier, and the voice of his master had whispered in his ear: "Sick'em!"

For a moment, with benign reproach, the Second Secretary regarded the unhappy page, and then addressed him with laborious sarcasm.

"James," he said, "people do not communicate with ambassadors in notes wrapped around half-crowns and hurled from windows. That is the way one corresponds with an organ-grinder." Ford sprang to his feet.

"And meanwhile," he exclaimed angrily, "the man will get away."

Without seeking permission, he ran past James, and through the empty outer offices. In two minutes he returned, herding before him an individual, seedy and soiled. In appearance the man suggested that in life his place was to

5

support a sandwich-board. Ford reluctantly relinquished his hold upon a folded paper which he laid in front of the Secretary.

"This man," he explained, "picked that out of the gutter in Sowell Street, It's not addressed to any one, so you read it!"

"I thought it was for the Ambassador!" said the Secretary.

The soiled person coughed deprecatingly, and pointed a dirty digit at the paper. "On the inside," he suggested. The paper was wrapped around a half-crown and folded in at each end. The diplomat opened it hesitatingly, but having read what was written, laughed.

"There's nothing in THAT," he exclaimed. He passed the note to Ford. The reporter fell upon it eagerly.

The note was written in pencil on an unruled piece of white paper. The handwriting was that of a woman. What Ford read was:

"I am a prisoner in the street on which this paper is found. The house faces east. I think I am on the top story. I was brought here three weeks ago. They are trying to kill me. My uncle, Charles Ralph Pearsall, is doing this to get my money. He is at Gerridge's Hotel in Craven Street, Strand. He will tell you I am insane. My name is Dosia Pearsall Dale. My home is at Dalesville, Kentucky, U. S. A. Everybody knows me there, and knows I am not insane. If you would save a life take this at once to the American Embassy, or to Scotland Yard. For God's sake, help me."

When he had read the note, Ford continue to study it. Until he was quite sure his voice would not betray his interest, he did not raise his eyes.

"Why," he asked, "did you say that there's nothing in this?"

"Because," returned the diplomat conclusively, "we got a note like that, or nearly like it, a week ago, and——"

Ford could not restrain a groan. "And you never told me!"

"There wasn't anything to tell," protested the diplomat. "We handed it over to the police, and they reported there was nothing in it. They couldn't find the man at that hotel, and, of course, they couldn't find the house with no more to go on than——"

"And so," exclaimed Ford rudely, "they decided there was no man, and no house!"

"Their theory," continued the Secretary patiently, "is that the girl is confined in one of the numerous private sanatoriums in Sowell Street, that she is insane, that because she's under restraint she IMAGINES the nurses are trying to kill her and that her relatives are after her money. Insane people are always thinking that. It's a very common delusion."

Ford's eyes were shining with a wicked joy. "So," he asked indifferently, "you don't intend to do anything further?"

"What do you want us to do?" cried his friend. "Ring every door-bell in Sowell Street and ask the parlor-maid if they're murdering a lady on the top story?"

"Can I keep the paper?" demanded Ford. "You can keep a copy of it," consented the Secretary. "But if you think you're on the track of a big newspaper sensation, I can tell you now you're not. That's the work of a crazy woman, or it's a hoax. You amateur detectives——"

Ford was already seated at the table, scribbling a copy of the message, and making marginal notes.

"Who brought the FIRST paper?" he interrupted.

"A hansom-cab driver."

"What became of HIM?" snapped the amateur detective.

The Secretary looked inquiringly at James. "He drove away," said James.

"He drove away, did he?"' roared Ford. "And that was a week ago! Ye gods! What about Dalesville, Kentucky? Did you cable any one there?"

The dignity of the diplomat was becoming ruffled.

"We did not!" he answered. "If it wasn't true that her uncle was at that hotel, it was probably equally untrue that she had friends in America."

"But," retorted his friend, "you didn't forget to cable the State Department that you all went in your evening clothes to bow to the new King? You didn't neglect to cable that, did you?"

"The State Department," returned the Secretary, with withering reproof, "does not expect us to crawl over the roofs of houses and spy down chimneys to see if by any chance an American citizen is being murdered."

"Well," exclaimed Ford, leaping to his feet and placing his notes in his pocket, "fortunately, my paper expects me to do just that, and if it didn't, I'd do it anyway. And that is exactly what I am going to do now! Don't tell the others in the Embassy, and, for Heaven's sake, don't tell the police. Jimmy, get me a taxi. And you," he commanded, pointing at the one who had brought the note, "are coming with me to Sowell Street, to show me where you picked up that paper."

On the way to Sowell Street Ford stopped at a newspaper agency, and paid for the insertion that afternoon of the same advertisement in three newspapers. It read: "If hansom-cab driver who last week carried note, found in street, to American Embassy will mail his address to X. X. X., care of GLOBE, he will be rewarded."

From the nearest post-office he sent to his paper the following cable: "Query our local correspondent, Dalesville, Kentucky, concerning Dosia Pearsall Dale. Is she of sound mind, is she heiress. Who controls her money, what her business relations with her uncle Charles Ralph Pearsall, what her present address. If any questions, say inquiries come from solicitors of Englishman who wants to marry her. Rush answer."

Sowell Street is a dark, dirty little thoroughfare, running for only one block, parallel to Harley Street. Like it, it is decorated with the brass plates of physicians and the red lamps of surgeons, but, just as the medical men in Harley Street, in keeping with that thoroughfare, are broad, open, and with nothing to conceal, so those of Sowell Street, like their hiding-place, shrink from observation, and their lives are as sombre, secret, and dark as the street itself.

Within two turns of it Ford dismissed the taxicab. Giving the soiled person a half-smoked cigarette, he told him to walk through Sowell Street, and when he reached the place where he had picked up the paper, to drop the cigarette as near that spot as possible. He then was to turn into Weymouth Street and wait until Ford joined him. At a distance of fifty feet Ford followed the man, and saw him, when in the middle of the block, without apparent hesitation, drop the cigarette. The house in front of which it fell was marked, like many others, by the brass plate of a doctor. As Ford passed it he hit the cigarette with his walking-stick, and drove it into an area. When he overtook the man, Ford handed him another cigarette. "To make sure," he said, "C4 go back and drop this in the place you found the paper." For a moment the man hesitated.

"I might as well tell you," Ford continued, "that I knocked that last cigarette so far from where you dropped it that you won't be able to use it as a guide. So, if you don't really know where you found the paper, you'll save my time by saying so." Instead of being confused by the test, the man was amused by it. He laughed appreciatively admitted. "You've caught me out fair, governor," "I want the 'arf-crown, and I dropped the cigarette as near the place as I could. But I can't do it again. It was this way," he explained. "I wasn't taking notice of the houses. I was walking along looking into the gutter for stumps. I see this paper wrapped about something round. 'It's a copper,' I thinks, 'jucked out of a winder to a organ-grinder.' I snatches it, and runs. I didn't take no time to look at the houses. But it wasn't so far from where I showed you; about the middle house in the street and on the left 'and side."

Ford had never considered the man as a serious element in the problem. He believed him to know as little of the matter as he professed to know. But it was essential he should keep that little to himself.

"No one will pay you for talking," Ford pointed out, "and I'll pay you to keep quiet. So, if you say nothing concerning that note, at the end of two weeks, I'll leave two pounds for you with James, at the Embassy."

The man, who believed Ford to be an agent of the police, was only too happy to escape on such easy terms. After Ford had given him a pound on account, they parted.

From Wimpole Street the amateur detective went to the nearest public telephone and called up Gerridge's Hotel. He considered his first step should be to discover if Mr. Pearsall was at that hotel, or had ever stopped there. When the 'phone was answered, he requested that a message be delivered to Mr. Pearsall.

"Please tell him," he asked, "that the clothes he ordered are ready to try on."

He was informed that no one by that name was at the hotel. In a voice of concern Ford begged to know when Mr. Pearsall had gone away, and had he left any address.

"He was with you three weeks ago," Ford insisted. "He's an American gentleman, and there was a lady with him. She ordered a riding-habit of us: the same time he was measured for his clothes."

After a short delay, the voice from the hotel replied that no one of the name of Pearsall had been at the hotel that winter.

In apparent great disgust Ford rang off, and took a taxicab to his rooms in Jermyn Street. There he packed a suit-case and drove to Gerridge's. It was a quiet, respectable, "old-established" house in Craven Street, a thoroughfare almost entirely given over to small family hotels much frequented by Americans.

After he had registered and had left his bag in his room, Ford returned to the office, and in an assured manner asked that a card on which he had written "Henry W. Page, Dalesville, Kentucky," should be taken to Mr. Pearsall.

In a tone of obvious annoyance the proprietor returned the card, saying that there was no one of that name in the hotel, and added that no such person had ever stopped there. Ford expressed the liveliest distress.

"He TOLD me I'd find him here," he protested., "he and his niece." With the garrulousness of the American abroad, he confided his troubles to the entire staff of the hotel. "We're from the same town," he explained. "That's why I must see him. He's the only man in London I know, and I've spent all my money. He said he'd give me some he owes me, as soon as I reached London. If I can't get it, I'll have to go home by Wednesday's steamer." And, complained bitterly, "I haven't seen the Tower, nor Westminster Abbey."

In a moment, Ford's anxiety to meet Mr. Pearsall was apparently lost in a wave of self-pity. In his disappointment he appealing, pathetic figure.

Real detectives and rival newspaper men, even while they admitted Ford obtained facts that were denied them, claimed that they were given him from charity. Where they bullied, browbeat, and administered a third degree, Ford was embarrassed, deprecatory, an earnest, ingenuous, wide-eyed child. What he called his "working" smile begged of you not to be cross with him. His simplicity was apparently so hopeless, his confidence in whomever he addressed so complete, that often even the man he was pursuing felt for him a pitying contempt. Now as he stood uncertainly in the hall of the hotel, his helplessness moved the proud lady clerk to shake her cylinders of false hair sympathetically, the German waiters to regard his predicament with respect; even the proprietor, Mr. Gerridge himself, was ill at ease. Ford returned to his room, on the second floor of the hotel, and sat down on the edge of the bed.

In connecting Pearsall with Gerridge's, both the police and himself had failed. Of this there were three possible explanations: that the girl who wrote the letter was in error, that the letter was a hoax, that the proprietor of the hotel, for some reason, was protecting Pearsall, and had deceived both Ford and Scotland Yard. On the other hand, without knowing why the girl believed Pearsall would be found at Gerridge's, it was reasonable to assume that in so thinking she had been purposely misled. The question was, should he or not dismiss Gerridge's as a possible clew, and at once devote himself to finding the house in Sowell Street? He decided for the moment at least, to leave Gerridge's out of his calculations, but, as an excuse for returning there, to still retain his room. He at once started toward Sowell Street, and in order to find out if any one from the hotel were following him, he set forth on foot. As soon as he made sure he was not spied upon, he covered the remainder of the distance in a cab.

He was acting on the supposition that the letter was no practical joke, but a genuine cry for help. Sowell Street was a scene set for such an adventure. It was narrow, mean-looking, the stucco house-fronts, soot-stained, cracked, and uncared-for, the steps broken and unwashed. As he entered it a cold rain was falling, and a yellow fog that rolled between the houses added to its dreariness. It was now late in the afternoon, and so overcast the sky that in many rooms the gas was lit and the curtains drawn.

The girl, apparently from observing the daily progress of the sun, had written she was on the west side of the street and, she believed, in an upper story. The man who picked up the note had said he had found it opposite the houses in the middle of the block. Accordingly, Ford proceeded on the supposition that the entire east side of the street, the lower stories of the west side, and the houses at each end were eliminated. The three houses in the centre of the row were outwardly alike. They were of four stories. Each was the residence of a physician, and in each, in the upper stories, the blinds were drawn. From the front there was nothing to be learned, and in the hope that the rear might furnish some clew, Ford hastened to Wimpole Street, in which the houses to the east backed upon those to the west in Sowell Street. These houses were given over to furnished lodgings, and under the pretext of renting chambers, it was easy for Ford to enter them, and from the apartments in the rear to obtain several hasty glimpses of the backs of the three houses in Sowell Street. But neither from this view-point did he gather any fact of interest. In one of the three houses in Sowell Street iron bars were fastened across the windows of the fourth floor, but in private sanatoriums this was neither unusual nor suspicious. The bars might cover the windows of a nursery to prevent children from falling out, or the room of some timid householder with a lively fear of burglars.

In a quarter of an hour Ford was again back in Sowell Street no wiser than when he had entered it. From the outside, at least, the three houses under suspicion gave no sign. In the problem before him there was one point that Ford found difficult to explain. It was the only one that caused him to question if the letter was genuine. What puzzled him was this: Why, if the girl were free to throw two notes from the window, did she not throw them out by the dozen? If she were able to reach a window, opening on the street, why did she not call for help? Why did she not, by hurling out every small article the room contained, by screams, by breaking the window-panes, attract a crowd, and, through it, the police? That she had not done so seemed to show that only at rare intervals was she free from restraint, or at liberty to enter the front room that opened on the street. Would it be equally difficult, Ford asked himself, for one in the street to communicate with her? What signal could he give that would draw an answering signal from the girl?

Standing at the corner, hidden by the pillars of a portico, the water dripping from his rain-coat, Ford gazed long and anxiously at the blank windows of the three houses. Like blind eyes staring into his, they told no tales, betrayed no secret. Around him the commonplace life of the neighborhood proceeded undisturbed. Somewhere concealed in the single row of houses a girl was imprisoned, her life threatened; perhaps even at that moment she was facing her death. While, on either side, shut from her by the thickness only of a brick wall, people were talking, reading, making tea, preparing the evening meal, or, in the street below, hurrying by, intent on trivial errands. Hansom cabs, prowling in search of a fare, passed through the street where a woman was being robbed of a fortune, the drivers occupied only with thoughts of a possible shilling; a housemaid with a jug in her hand and a shawl over her bare head, hastened to the near-by public-house; the postman made his rounds, and delivered comic postal-cards; a policeman, shedding water from his shining cape, halted, gazed severely at the sky, and, unconscious of the crime that was going forward within the sound of his own footsteps, continued stolidly into Wimpole Street.

A hundred plans raced through Ford's brain; he would arouse the street with a false alarm of fire and lead the firemen, with the tale of a smoking chimney, to one of the three houses; he would feign illness, and, taking refuge in one of them, at night would explore the premises; he would impersonate a detective, and insist upon his right to search for stolen property. As he rejected these and a dozen schemes as fantastic, his brain and eyes were still alert for any chance advantage that the street might offer. But the minutes passed into an hour, and no one had entered any of the three houses, no one had left them. In the lower stories, from behind the edges of the blinds, lights appeared, but of the life within there was no sign. Until he hit upon a plan of action, Ford felt there was no longer anything to be gained by remaining in Sowell Street. Already the answer to his cable might have arrived at his rooms; at Gerridge's he might still learn something of Pearsall. He decided to revisit both these places, and, while so engaged, to send from his office one of his assistants to cover the Sowell Street houses. He cast a last, reluctant look at the closed blinds, and moved away. As he did so, two itinerant musicians dragging behind them a small street piano on wheels turned the corner, and, as the rain had now ceased, one of them pulled the oil-cloth covering from the instrument and, seating himself on a camp-stool at the curb, opened the piano. After a discouraged glance at the darkened windows, the other, in a hoarse, strident tenor, to the accompaniment of the piano, began to sing. The voice of the man was raucous, penetrating. It would have reached the recesses of a tomb.

"She sells sea-shells on the sea-shore," the vocalist wailed. "The shells she sells are sea-shells, I'm sure."

The effect was instantaneous. A window was flung open, and an indignant householder with one hand frantically waved the musicians away, and with the other threw them a copper coin.

At the same moment Ford walked quickly to the piano and laid a half-crown on top of it.

"Follow me to Harley Street," he commanded. "Don't hurry. Take your time. I want you to help me in a sort of practical joke. It's worth a sovereign to you."

He passed on quickly. When he glanced behind him, he saw the two men, fearful lest the promised fortune might escape them, pursuing him at a trot. At Harley Street they halted, breathless.

"How long," Ford demanded of the one who played the piano, "will it take you to learn the accompaniment to a new song?"

"While you're whistling it," answered the man eagerly.

"And I'm as quick at a tune as him," assured the other anxiously. "I can sing——"

"You cannot," interrupted Ford. "I'm going to do the singing myself. Where is there a public-house near here where we can hire a back room, and rehearse?"

Half an hour later, Ford and the piano-player entered Sowell Street dragging the piano behind them. The amateur detective still wore his rain-coat, but his hat he had exchanged for a cap, and, instead of a collar, he had knotted around his bare neck a dirty kerchief. At the end of the street they halted, and in some embarrassment Ford raised his voice in the chorus of a song well known in the music-halls. It was a very good voice, much too good for "open-air work," as his companion had already assured him, but, what was of chief importance to Ford, it carried as far as he wished it to go. Already in Wimpole Street four coins of the realm, flung to him from the highest windows, had testified to its power. From the end of Sowell Street Ford moved slowly from house to house until he was directly opposite the three in one of which he believed the girl to be. "We will try the NEW songs here," he said.

Night had fallen, and, except for the gas-lamps, the street was empty, and in such darkness that even without his disguise Ford ran no risk of recognition. His plan was not new. It dated from the days of Richard the Lion-hearted. But if the prisoner were alert and intelligent, even though she could make no answer, Ford believed through his effort she would gain courage, would grasp that from the outside a friend was working toward her. All he knew of the prisoner was that she came from Kentucky. Ford fixed his eyes on the houses opposite, and cleared his throat. The man struck the opening chords, and in a high barytone, and in a cockney accent that made even the accompanist grin, Ford lifted his voice.

"The sun shines bright on my old Kentucky home," he sang; "'tis summer, and the darkies are gay."

He finished the song, but there was no sign. For all the impression he had made upon Sowell Street, he might have been singing in his chambers. "And now the other," commanded Ford.

The house-fronts echoed back the cheering notes of "Dixie." Again Ford was silent, and again The silence answered him. The accompanist glared disgustedly at the darkened windows.

"They don't know them songs," he explained professionally. "Give 'em, 'Mollie Married the Marquis.'"

"I'll sing the first one again," said Ford. Once more he broke into the pathetic cadences of the "Old Kentucky Home." But there was no response. He was beginning to feel angry, absurd. He believed he had wasted precious moments, and, even as he sang, his mind was already working upon a new plan. The song ceased, unfinished.

"It's no use!" he exclaimed. Remembering himself, he added: "We'll try the next street."

But even as he spoke he leaped forward. Coming apparently from nowhere, something white sank through the semi-darkness and fell at his feet. It struck the pavement directly in front of the middle one of the three houses. Ford fell upon it and clutched it in both hands. It was a woman's glove. Ford raced back to the piano.

"Once more," he cried, "play 'Dixie'!"

He shouted out the chorus exultantly, triumphantly. Had he spoken it in words, the message could not have carried more clearly.

Ford now believed he had found the house, found the woman, and was eager only to get rid of his companion and, in his own person, return to Sowell Street. But, lest the man might suspect there was in his actions something more serious than a practical joke, he forced himself to sing the new songs in three different streets. Then, pretending to tire of his prank, he paid the musician and left him. He was happy, exultant, tingling with excitement. Good-luck had been with him, and, hoping that Gerridge's might yet yield some clew to Pearsall, he returned there. Calling up the London office of the REPUBLIC, he directed that one of his assistants, an English lad named Cuthbert, should at once join him at that hotel. Cuthbert was but just out of Oxford. He wished to become a writer of fiction, and, as a means of seeing many kinds of life at first hand, was in training as a "Pressman." His admiration for Ford amounted to almost hero-worship; and he regarded an "assignment" with his chief as a joy and an honor. Full of enthusiasm, and as soon as a taxicab could bring him, he arrived at Gerridge's, where, in a corner of the deserted coffee-room, Ford explained the situation. Until he could devise a way to enter the Sowell Street house. Cuthbert was to watch over it.

"The number of the house is forty," Ford told him; "the name on the door-plate, Dr. Prothero. Find out everything you can about him without letting any one catch you at it. Better begin at the nearest chemist's. Say you are on the verge of a nervous breakdown, and ask the man to mix you a sedative, and recommend a physician. Show him Prothero's name and address on a piece of paper, and say Prothero has been recommended to you as a specialist on nervous troubles. Ask what he thinks of him. Get him to talk. Then visit the trades-people and the public-houses in the neighborhood, and say you are from some West End shop where Prothero, wants to open an account. They may talk, especially if his credit is bad. And, if you find out enough about him to give me a working basis, I'll try to get into the house to-night. Meanwhile, I'm going to make another quick search of this hotel for Pearsall. I'm not satisfied he has not been here. For why should Miss Dale, with all the hotels in London to choose from, have named this particular one, unless she had good reason for it? Now, go, and meet me in an hour in Sowell Street."

Cuthbert was at the door when he remembered he had brought with him from the office Ford's mail and cablegrams. Among the latter was the one for which Ford had asked.

"Wait," he commanded. "This is about the girl. You had better know what it says." The cable read:

"Girl orphan, Dalesville named after her family, for three generations mill-owners, father died four years ago, Pearsall brother-in-law until she is twenty-one, which will be in three months. Girl well known, extremely popular, lived Dalesville until last year, when went abroad with uncle, since then reports of melancholia and nervous prostration, before that health excellent—no signs insanity—none in family. Be careful how handle Pearsall, was doctor, gave up practice to look after estate, is prominent in local business and church circles, best reputation, beware libel."

For the benefit of Cuthbert, Ford had been reading the cable aloud. The last paragraph seemed especially to interest him, and he read it twice, the second time slowly, and emphasizing the word "doctor."

"A doctor!" he repeated. "Do you see where that leads us? It may explain several things. The girl was in good health until went abroad with her uncle, and he is a medical man."

The eyes of Cuthbert grew wide with excitement.

"You mean poison!" he whispered. "Slow poison!"

"Beware libel," laughed Ford nervously, his own eyes lit with excitement. "Suppose," he exclaimed, "he has been using arsenic? He would have many opportunities, and it's colorless, tasteless; and arsenic would account for her depression and melancholia. The time when he must turn over her money is very near, and, suppose he has spent the money, speculated with it, and lost it, or that he still has it and wants to keep it? In three months she will be of age, and he must make an accounting. The arsenic does not work fast enough. So what does he do? To save himself from exposure, or to keep the money, he throws her into this private sanatorium, to make away with her."

Ford had been talking in an eager whisper. While he spoke his cigar had ceased to burn, and to light it, from a vase on the mantel he took a spill, one of those spirals of paper that in English hotels, where the proprietor is of a frugal mind, are still used to prevent extravagance in matches. Ford lit the spill at the coal fire, and with his cigar puffed at the flame. As he did so the paper unrolled. To the astonishment of Cuthbert, Ford clasped it in both hands, blotted out the tiny flame, and, turning quickly to a table, spread out the charred paper flat. After one quick glance, Ford ran to the fireplace, and, seizing a handfull of the spills, began rapidly to unroll them. Then he turned to Cuthbert and, without speaking, showed him the charred spill. It was a scrap torn from the front page of a newspaper. The half-obliterated words at which Ford pointed were DALESVILLE COUR

———

"His torn paper!" said Ford. "The DALESVILLE COURIER. Pearsall HAS been in this hotel!" He handed another spill to Cuthbert.

"From that one," said Ford, "we get the date, December 3. Allowing three weeks for the newspaper to reach London, Pearsall must have seen it just three weeks ago, just when Miss Dale says he was in the hotel. The landlord has lied to me."

Ford rang for a waiter, and told him to ask Mr. Gerridge to come to the smoking-room.

As Cuthbert was leaving it, Gerridge was entering it, and Ford was saying:

"It seems you've been lying to the police and to me. Unless you desire to be an accessory to a murder, You had better talk quick!"

An hour later Ford passed slowly through Sowell Street in a taxicab, and, finding Cuthbert on guard, signalled him to follow. In Wimpole Street the cab drew up to the curb, and Cuthbert entered it.

"I have found Pearsall," said Ford. "He is in No. 40 with Prothero."

He then related to Cuthbert what had happened. Gerridge had explained that when the Police called, his first thought was to protect the good name of his hotel. He had denied any knowledge of Pearsall only because he no longer was a guest, and, as he supposed Pearsall had passed out of his life, he saw no reason, why, through an arrest and a scandal, his hotel should be involved. Believing Ford to be in the secret service of the police, he was now only too anxious to clear himself of suspicion by telling all he knew. It was but little. Pearsall and his niece had been at the hotel for three days. During that time the niece, who appeared to be an invalid, remained in her room. On the evening of the third day, while Pearsall was absent, a call from him had come for her by telephone, on receiving which Miss Dale had at once left the hotel, apparently in great agitation. That night she did not return, but in the morning Pearsall came to collect his and her luggage and to settle his account. He explained that a woman relative living at the Langham Hotel had been taken suddenly ill, and had sent for him and his niece. Her condition had been so serious that they had remained with her all night, and his niece still was at her bedside. The driver of a four-wheeler, who for years had stood on the cab-rank in front of Gerridge's, had driven Pearsall to the Langham. This man was at the moment on the rank, and from him Ford learned what he most wished to know.

The cabman remembered Pearsall, and having driven him to the Langham, for the reason that immediately after setting him down there, and while "crawling" for a fare in Portland Place, a whistle from the Langham had recalled him, and the same luggage that had just been taken from the top of his cab was Put back on it, and he was directed by the porter of the hotel to take it to a house in Sowell Street. There a man-servant had helped him unload the trunks and had paid him his fare. The cabman did not remember the number of the house, but knew it was on the west side of the street and in the middle of the block.

Having finished with Gerridge and the cab-man, Ford had at once gone to the Langham Hotel, where, as he anticipated, nothing was known of Pearsall or his niece, or of any invalid lady. But the hall-porter remembered the American gentleman who had driven up with many pieces of luggage, and who, although it was out of season, and many suites in the hotel were vacant, had found none to suit him. He had then set forth on foot, having left word that his trunks be sent after him. The address he gave was a house in Sowell Street.

The porter recalled the incident because he and the cabman had grumbled over the fact that in five minutes they had twice to handle the same boxes.

"It is pretty evident," said Ford, what Pearsall had in mind, but chance was against him. He thought when he had unloaded his trunks at the Langham and dismissed the cabman he had destroyed the link connecting him with Gerridge's. He could not foresee that the same cabman would be loitering in the neighborhood. He should have known that four-wheelers are not as plentiful as they once were; and he should have given that particular one more time to get away. His idea in walking to the Sowell Street house was obviously to prevent the new cabman from seeing him enter it. But, just where he thought he was clever, was just where he tripped. If he had remained with his trunks he would have seen that the cabman was the same one who had brought them and him from Craven Street, and he would have given any other address in London than the one he did.

"And now," said Ford, "that we have Pearsall where we want him, tell me what you have learned about Prothero?"

Cuthbert smiled importantly, and produced a piece of paper scribbled over with notes.

"Prothero," he said, "seems to be THIS sort of man. If he made your coffee for you, before you tasted it, you'd like him to drink a cup of it first."

II

"Prothero," said Cuthbert, "is a man of mystery. As soon as I began asking his neighbors questions, I saw he was of interest and that I was of interest. I saw they did not believe I was an agent of a West End shop, but a detective. So they wouldn't talk at all, or else they talked freely. And from one of them, a chemist named Needham, I got all I wanted. He's had a lawsuit against Prothero, and hates him. Prothero got him to invest in a medicine to cure the cocaine habit. Needham found the cure was no cure, but cocaine disguised. He sued for his money, and during the trial the police brought in Prothero's record. Needham let me copy it, and it seems to embrace every crime except treason. The man is a Russian Jew. He was arrested and prosecuted in Warsaw, Vienna, Berlin, Belgrade; all over Europe, until finally the police drove him to America. There he was an editor of an anarchist paper, a blackmailer, a 'doctor' of hypnotism, a clairvoyant, and a professional bigamist. His game was to open rooms as a clairvoyant, and advise silly women how to invest their money. When he found out which of them had the most money, he would marry her, take over her fortune, and skip. In Chicago, he was tried for poisoning one wife, and the trial brought out the fact that two others had died under suspicious circumstances, and that there were three

30

more unpoisoned but anxious to get back their money. He was sentenced to ten years for bigamy, but pardoned because he was supposed to be insane, and dying. Instead of dying, he opened a sanatorium in New York to cure victims of the drug habit. In reality, it was a sort of high-priced opium-den. The place was raided, and he jumped his bail and came to this country. Now he is running this private hospital in Sowell Street. Needham says it's a secret rendezvous for dope fiends. But they are very high-class dope fiends, who are willing to pay for seclusion, and the police can't get at him. I may add that he's tall and muscular, with a big black beard, and hands that could strangle a bull. In Chicago, during the poison trial, the newspapers called him 'the Modern Bluebeard.'"

For a short time Ford was silent. But, in the dark corner of the cab, Cuthbert could see that his cigar was burning briskly.

"Your friend seems a nice chap," said Ford at last. "Calling on him will be a real pleasure. I especially like what you say about his hands."

"I have a plan," began the assistant timidly, "a plan to get you into the house-if you don't mind my making suggestions?"

"Not at all!" exclaimed his chief heartily.

"Get me into the house by all means; that's what we're here for. The fact that I'm to be poisoned or strangled after I get there mustn't discourage us.'"

"I thought," said Cuthbert, "I might stand guard outside, while you got in as a dope fiend."

Ford snorted indignantly. "Do I LOOK like a dope fiend?" he protested.

The voice of the assistant was one of discouragement.

"You certainly do not," he exclaimed regretfully. "But it's the only plan I could think of."

"It seems to me," said his chief testily, "that you are not so very healthy-looking yourself. What's the matter with YOUR getting inside as a dope fiend and MY standing guard?"

"But I wouldn't know what to do after I got inside," complained the assistant, "and you would. You are so clever."

The expression of confidence seemed to flatter Ford.

"I might do this," he said. "I might pretend I was recovering from a heavy spree, and ask to be taken care of until I am sober. Or I could be a very good imitation of a man on the edge of a nervous breakdown. I haven't been five years in the newspaper business without knowing all there is to know about nerves. That's it!" he cried. "I will do that! And if Mr. Bluebeard Svengali, the Strangler of Paris person, won't take me in as a patient, we'll come back with a couple of axes and BREAK in. But we'll try the nervous breakdown first, and we'll try it now. I will be a naval officer," declared Ford. "I made the round-the-world cruise with our fleet as a correspondent, and I know enough sea slang to fool a medical man. I am a naval officer whose nerves have gone wrong. I have heard of his sanatorium through——" "How," asked Ford sharply, "have I heard of his sanatorium?"

"You saw his advertisement in the DAILY WORLD," prompted Cuthbert. "'Home of convalescents; mental and nervous troubles cured.'"

"And," continued Ford, "I have come to him for rest and treatment. My name is Lieutenant Henry Grant. I arrived in London two weeks ago on the MAURETANIA. But my name was not on the passenger-list, because I did not want the Navy Department to know I was taking my leave abroad. I have been stopping at my own address in Jermyn Street, and my references are yourself, the Embassy, and my landlord. You will telephone him at once that, if any one asks after Henry Grant, he is to say what you tell him to say. And if any one sends for Henry Grant's clothes, he is to send MY clothes."

"But you don't expect to be in there as long as that?" exclaimed Cuthbert.

"I do not," said Ford. "But, if he takes me in, I must make a bluff of sending for my things. No; either I will be turned out in five minutes, or if he accepts me as a patient I will be there until midnight. If I cannot get the girl out of the house by midnight, it will mean that I can't get out myself, and you had better bring the police and the coroner."

"Do you mean it?" asked Cuthbert.

"I most certainly do!" exclaimed Ford.

"Until twelve I want a chance to get this story exclusively for our paper. If she is not free by then it means I have fallen down on it, and you and the police are to begin to batter in the doors."

The two young men left the cab, and at some distance from each other walked to Sowell Street. At the house of Dr. Prothero, Ford stopped and rang the bell. From across the street Cuthbert saw the door open and the figure of a man of almost gigantic stature block the doorway. For a moment he stood there, and then Cuthbert saw him step to one side, saw Ford enter the house and the door close upon him. Cuthbert at once ran to a telephone, and, having instructed Ford's landlord as to the part he was to play, returned to Sowell Street. There, in a state nearly approaching a genuine nervous breakdown, he continued his vigil.

Even without his criminal record to cast a glamour over him, Ford would have found Dr. Prothero, a disturbing person. His size was enormous, his eyes piercing, sinister, unblinking, and the hands that could strangle a bull, and with which as though to control himself, he continually pulled at his black beard, were gigantic, of a deadly white, with fingers long and prehensile. In his manner he had all the suave insolence of the Oriental and the suspicious alertness of one constantly on guard, but also, as Ford at once noted, of one wholly without fear. He had not been over a moment in his presence before the reporter felt that to successfully lie to such a man might be counted as a triumph.

Prothero opened the door into a little office leading off the hall, and switched on the electric lights. For some short time, without any effort to conceal his suspicion, he stared at Ford in silence.

"Well?" he said, at last. His tone was a challenge.

Ford had already given his assumed name and profession, and he now ran glibly into the story he had planned. He opened his card-case and looked into it doubtfully. "I find I have no card with me," he said; "but I am, as I told you, Lieutenant Grant, of the United States Navy. I am all right physically, except for my nerves. They've played me a queer trick. If the facts get out at home, it might cost me my commission. So I've come over here for treatment."

"Why to ME?" asked Prothero.

"I saw by your advertisement," said the reporter, "that you treated for nervous mental troubles. Mine is an illusion," he went on. "I see things, or, rather, always one thing-a battle-ship coming at us head on. For the last year I've been executive officer of the KEARSARGE, and the responsibility has been too much for me."

35

"You see a battle-ship?" inquired the Jew.

"A phantom battle-ship," Ford explained, "a sort OF FLYING DUTCHMAN. The time I saw it I was on the bridge, and I yelled and telegraphed the engine-room. I brought the ship to a full stop, and backed her. But it was dirty weather, and the error was passed over. After that, when I saw the thing coming I did nothing. But each time I think it is real." Ford shivered slightly and glanced about him. "Some day," he added fatefully, "it WILL be real, and I will NOT signal, and the ship will sink!"

In silence, Prothero observed his visitor closely. The young man seemed sincere, genuine. His manner was direct and frank. He looked the part he had assumed, as one used to authority.

"My fees are large," said the Russian.

At this point, had Ford, regardless of terms, exhibited a hopeful eagerness to at once close with him, the Jew would have shown him the door. But Ford was on guard, and well aware that a lieutenant in the navy had but few guineas to throw away on medicines. He made a movement as though to withdraw.

"Then I am afraid," he said, "I must go somewhere else."

His reluctance apparently only partially satisfied the Jew.

Ford adopted opposite tactics. He was never without ready money. His paper saw to it that in its interests he was always able at any moment to pay for a special train across Europe, or to bribe the entire working staff of a cable office. From his breast-pocket he took a blue linen envelope, and allowed the Jew to see that it was filled with twenty-pound notes. "I have means outside my pay," said Ford.

"I would give almost any price to the man who can cure me." The eyes of the Russian flashed avariciously.

"I will arrange the terms to suit you," he exclaimed. "Your case interests me. Do you See this mirage only at sea?"

"In any open place," Ford assured him. "In a park or public square, but of course most frequently at sea."

The quack waved his great hands as though brushing aside a curtain.

"I will remove the illusion," he said, "and give you others more pretty." He smiled meaningfully—an evil, leering smile. "When will you come?" he asked. Ford glanced about him nervously.

"I shall stay now," he said. "I confess, in the streets and in my lodgings I am frightened. You give me confidence. I want to stay near you. I feel safe with you. If you will give me writing-paper, I will send for my things."

For a moment the Jew hesitated, and then motioned to a desk. As Ford wrote, Prothero stood near him, and the reporter knew that over his shoulder the Jew was reading what he wrote. Ford gave him the note, unsealed, and asked that it be forwarded at once to his lodgings.

"To-morrow," he said, "I will call up our Embassy, and give my address to our Naval Attache."

"I will attend to that," said Prothero.

"From now you are in my hands, and you can communicate with the outside only through me. You are to have absolute rest—no books, no letters, no papers. And you will be fed from a spoon. I will explain my treatment later. You will now go to your room, and you will remain there until you are a well man."

Ford had no wish to be at once shut off from the rest of the house. The odor of cooking came through the hall, and seemed to offer an excuse for delay.

"I smell food," he laughed. "And I'm terrifically hungry. Can't I have a farewell dinner before you begin feeding me from a spoon?"

The Jew was about to refuse, but, with his guilty knowledge of what was going forward in the house, he could not be too sure of those he allowed to enter it. He wanted more time to spend in studying this new patient, and the dinner-table seemed to offer a place where he could do so without the other suspecting he was under observation.

"My associate and I were just about to dine," he said. "You will wait here until I have another place laid, and you can join us."

He departed, walking heavily down the hall, but almost at once Ford, whose ears were alert for any sound, heard him returning, approaching stealthily on tiptoe. If by this maneuver the Jew had hoped to discover his patient in some indiscretion, he was unsuccessful, for he found Ford standing just where he had left him, with his back turned to the door, and gazing with apparent interest at a picture on the wall. The significance of the incident was not lost upon the intruder. It taught him he was still under surveillance, and that he must bear himself warily. Murmuring some excuse for having returned, the Jew again departed, and in a few minutes Ford heard his voice, and that of another man, engaged in low tones in what was apparently an eager argument.

Only once was the voice of the other man raised sufficiently for Ford to distinguish his words. "He is an American," protested the voice; "that makes it worse."

Ford guessed that the speaker was Pearsall, and that against his admittance to the house he was making earnest protest. A door, closing with a bang, shut off the argument, but within a few minutes it was evident the Jew had carried his point, for he reappeared to announce that dinner was waiting. It was served in a room at the farther end of the hall, and at the table, which was laid for three, Ford found a man already seated. Prothero introduced him as "my associate," but from his presence in the house, and from the fact that he was an American, Ford knew that he was Pearsall.

Pearsall was a man of fifty. He was tall, spare, with closely shaven face and gray hair, worn rather long. He spoke with the accent of a Southerner, and although to Ford he was studiously polite, he was obviously greatly ill at ease. He had the abrupt, inattentive manners, the trembling fingers and quivering lips, of one who had long been a slave to the drug habit, and who now, with difficulty, was holding himself in hand.

Throughout the dinner, speaking to him as though, interested only as his medical advisers, the Jew, and occasionally the American, sharply examined and cross-examined their visitor. But they were unable to trip him in his story, or to suggest that he was not just what he claimed to be.

When the dinner was finished, the three men, for different reasons, were each more at his ease. Both Pearsall and Prothero believed from the new patient they had nothing to fear, and Ford was congratulating himself that his presence at the house was firmly secure.

"I think," said Pearsall, "we should warn Mr. Grant that there are in the house other patients who, like himself, are suffering from nervous disorders. At times some silly neurotic woman becomes hysterical, and may make an outcry or scream. He must not think ——"

"That's all right!" Ford reassured him cheerfully. "I expect that. In a sanatorium it must be unavoidable."

As he spoke, as though by a signal prearranged, there came from the upper portion of the house a scream, long, insistent.

It was the voice of a woman, raised in appeal, in protest, shaken with fear. Without for an instant regarding it, the two men fastened their eyes upon the visitor. The hand of the Jew dropped quickly from his beard, and slid to the inside pocket of his coat. With eyes apparently unseeing, Ford noted the movement.

"He carries a gun," was his mental comment, "and he seems perfectly willing to use it." Aloud, he said: "That, I suppose is one of them?"

Prothero nodded gravely, and turned to Pearsall. "Will you attend her?" he asked.

As Pearsall rose and left the room, Prothero rose also.

"You will come with me," he directed, "and I will see you settle in your apartment. Your bag has arrived and is already there."

The room to which the Jew led him was the front one on the second story. It was in no way in keeping with a sanatorium, or a rest-cure. The walls were hidden by dark blue hangings, in which sparkled tiny mirrors, the floor was covered with Turkish rugs, the lights concealed inside lamps of dull brass bedecked with crimson tassels. In the air were the odors of stale tobacco-smoke, of cheap incense, and the sickly, sweet smell of opium. To Ford the place suggested a cigar-divan rather than a bedroom, and he guessed, correctly, that when Prothero had played at palmistry and clairvoyance this had been the place where he received his dupes. But the American expressed himself pleased with his surroundings, and while Prothero remained in the room, busied himself with unpacking his bag.

On leaving him the Jew halted in the door and delivered himself of a little speech. His voice was stern, sharp, menacing.

"Until you are cured," he said, "you will not put your foot outside this room. In this house are other inmates who, as you have already learned, are in a highly nervous state. The brains of some are unbalanced. With my associate and myself they are familiar, but the sight of a stranger roaming through the halls might upset them. They might attack you, might do you bodily injury. If you wish for anything, ring the electric bell beside your bed and an attendant will come. But you yourself must not leave the room."

He closed the door, and Ford, seating himself in front of the coal fire, hastily considered his position. He could not persuade himself that, strategically, it was a satisfactory one. The girl he sought was on the top or fourth floor, he on the second. To reach her he would have to pass through Well-lighted halls, up two flights Of stairs and try to enter a door that would undoubtedly be locked. On the other hand, instead of wandering about in the rain outside the house, he was now established on the inside, and as an inmate. Had there been time for a siege, he would have been confident of success. But there was no time. The written call for help had been urgent. Also, the scream he had heard, while the manner of the two men had shown that to them it was a commonplace, was to him a spur to instant action. In haste he knew there was the risk of failure, but he must take that risk.

He wished first to assure himself that Cuthbert was within call, and to that end put out the lights and drew aside the curtains that covered the window. Outside, the fog was rolling between the house-fronts, both rain and snow were falling heavily, and a solitary gas-lamp showed only a deserted and dripping street. Cautiously Ford lit a match and for an instant let the flame flare. He was almost at once rewarded by the sight of an answering flame that flickered from a dark doorway. Ford closed the window, satisfied that his line of communication with the outside world was still intact. The faithful Cuthbert was on guard.

Ford rapidly reviewed each possible course of action. These were several, but to lead any one of them to success, he saw that he must possess a better acquaintance with the interior of the house. Especially was it important that he should obtain a line of escape other than the one down the stairs to the front door. The knowledge that in the rear of the house there was a means of retreat by a servants' stairway, or over the roof of an adjoining building, or by a friendly fire-escape, would at least, lend him confidence in his adventure. Accordingly, in spite of Prothero's threat, he determined at once to reconnoitre. In case of his being discovered outside his room, he would explain his electric bell was out of order, that when he rang no servant had answered, and that he had sallied forth in search of one. To make this plausible, he unscrewed the cap of the electric button in the wall, and with his knife cut off enough of the wire to prevent a proper connection. He then replaced the cap and, opening the door, stepped into the hall.

The upper part of the house was, sunk in silence, but rising from the dining-room below, through the opening made by the stairs, came the voices of Prothero and Pearsall. And mixed with their voices came also the sharp hiss of water issuing from a siphon. The sound was reassuring. Apparently, over their whiskey-and-soda the two men were still lingering at the dinner-table. For the moment, then—so far, at least, as they were concerned—the coast was clear.

Stepping cautiously, and keeping close to the wall, Ford ran lightly up the stairs to the hall of the third floor. It was lit brightly by a gas-jet, but no one was in sight, and the three doors opening upon it were shut. At the rear of the hall was a window; the blind was raised, and through the panes, dripping in the rain, Ford caught a glimpse of the rigid iron rods of a fire-escape. His spirits leaped exultantly. If necessary, by means of this scaling ladder, he could work entirely from the outside. Greatly elated, he tiptoed past the closed doors and mounted to the fourth floor. This also was lit by a gas-jet that showed at one end of the hall a table on which were medicine-bottles and a tray covered by a napkin; and at the other end, piled upon each other and blocking the hall-window, were three steamer-trunks. Painted on each were the initials, "D. D." Ford breathed an exclamation.

"Dosia Dale," he muttered, "I have found you!" He was again confronted by three closed doors, one leading to a room that faced the street, another opening upon a room in the rear of the house, and opposite, across the hallway, still another door. He observed that the first two doors were each fastened from the outside by bolts and a spring lock, and that the key to each lock was in place. The fact moved him with indecision. If he took possession of the keys, he could enter the rooms at his pleasure. On the other hand, should their loss be discovered, an alarm would be raised and he would inevitably come under suspicion. The very purpose he had in view might be frustrated. He decided that where they were the keys would serve him as well as in his pocket, and turned his attention to the third door. This was not locked, and, from its position, Ford guessed it must be an entrance to a servants' stairway.

Confident of this, he opened it, and found a dark, narrow landing, a flight of steps mounting from the kitchen below, and, to his delight an iron ladder leading to a trap-door. He could hardly forego a cheer. If the trap-door were not locked, he had found a third line of retreat, a means of escape by way of the roof, far superior to any he might attempt by the main staircase and the street-door.

Ford stepped into the landing, closing the door behind him and though this left him in complete darkness, he climbed the ladder, and with eager fingers felt for the fastenings of the trap. He had feared to find a padlock, but, to his infinite relief, his fingers closed upon two bolts. Noiselessly, and smoothly, they drew back from their sockets. Under the pressure of his hand the trap door lifted, and through the opening swept a breath of chill night air.

Ford hooked one leg over a round of the ladder and, with hands frees moved the trap to one side. An instant later he had scrambled to the roof, and, after carefully replacing the trap, rose and looked about him. To his satisfaction, he found that the roof upon which he stood ran level with the roofs adjoining its to as far as Devonshire Street, where they encountered the wall of an apartment house. This was of seven stories. On the fifth story a row of windows, brilliantly lighted, opened upon the roofs over which he planned to make his retreat. Ford chuckled with nervous excitement.

"Before long," he assured himself, "I will be visiting the man who owns that flat. He will think I am a burglar. He will send for the police. There is no one in the world I shall be so glad to see!"

Ford considered that running over roofs, even when their pitfalls were not concealed by a yellow fog, was an awkward exercise, and decided that before he made his dash for freedom, the part of a careful jockey would be to take a preliminary canter over the course. Accordingly, among party walls of brick, rain-pipes, chimney-pipes, and telephone wires, he felt his way to the wall of the apartment house; and then, with a clearer idea of the obstacles to be avoided, raced back to the point whence he had started.

Next, to discover the exact position of the fire-escape, he dropped to his knees and crawled to the rear edge of the roof. The light from the back windows of the fourth floor showed him an iron ladder from the edge of the roof to the platform of the fire-escape, and the platform itself, stretching below the windows the width of the building. He gave a sigh of satisfaction, but the same instant exclaimed with dismay. The windows opening upon the fire-escape were closely barred. For a moment he was unable to grasp why a fire-escape should be placed where escape was impossible, until he recognized that the ladder must have been erected first and the iron bars later; probably only since Miss Dale had been made a prisoner.

But he now appreciated that in spite of the iron bars he was nearer that prisoner than he had ever been. Should he return to the hall below, even while he could unlock the doors, he was in danger of discovery by those inside the house. But from the fire-escape only a window-pane would separate him from the prisoner, and though the bars would keep him at arm's-length, he might at least speak with her, and assure her that her call for help had carried. He grasped the sides of the ladder and dropped to the platform. As he had already seen that the window farthest to the left was barricaded with trunks, he disregarded it, and passed quickly to the two others. Behind both of these, linen shades were lowered, but, to his relief, he found that in the middle window the lower sash, as though for ventilation, was slightly raised, leaving an opening of a few inches. Kneeling on the gridiron platform of the fire-escape, and pressing his face against the bars, he brought his eyes level with this opening. Owing to the lowered window-blind, he could see nothing in the room, nor could he distinguish any sound until above the drip and patter of the rain there came to him the peaceful ticking of a clock and the rattle of coal falling to the fender. But of any sound that was human there was none. That the room was empty, and that the girl was in the front of the house was possible, and the temptation to stretch his hand through the bars and lift the blind was almost compelling. If he did so, and the girl were inside, she might make an outcry, or, guarding her, there might be an attendant, who at once would sound the alarm. The risk was evident, but, encouraged by the silence, Ford determined to take the chance. Slipping one hand between the bars he caught the end of the blind, and, pulling it gently down, let the spring draw it upward. Through an opening of six inches the room lay open before him. He saw a door leading to another room, at one side an iron cot, and in front of the coal fire, facing him, a girl seated in a deep arm-chair. A book lay on her knees, and she was intently reading.

The girl was young, and her face, in spite of an unnatural pallor and an expression of deep melancholy, was one of extreme beauty. She wore over a night-dress a long loose wrapper corded at the waist, and, as though in readiness for the night, her black hair had been drawn back into smooth, heavy braids. She made so sweet and sad a picture that Ford forgot his errand, forgot his damp and chilled body, and for a moment in sheer delight knelt, with his face pressed close to the bars, and gazed at her.

A movement on the part of the girl brought him to his senses. She closed the book, and, leaning forward, rested her chin upon the hollow of her hand and stared into the fire. Her look was one of complete and hopeless misery. Ford did not hesitate. The girl was alone, but that at any moment an

49

attendant might join her was probable, and the rare chance that now offered would be lost. He did not dare to speak, or by any sound attract her attention, but from his breast-pocket he took the glove thrown to him from the window, and, with a jerk, tossed it through the narrow opening. It fell directly at her feet. She had not seen the glove approach, but the slight sound it made in falling caused her to start and turn her eyes toward it. Through the window, breathless, and with every nerve drawn taut, Ford watched her.

For a moment, partly in alarm, partly in bewilderment, she sat motionless, regarding the glove with eyes fixed and staring. Then she lifted them to the ceiling, in quick succession to each of the closed doors, and then to the window. In his race across the roofs Ford had lacked the protection of a hat, and his hair was plastered across his forehead; his face was streaked with soot and snow, his eyes shone with excitement. But at sight of this strange apparition the girl made no sign. Her alert mind had in an instant taken in the significance of the glove, and for her what followed could have but one meaning. She knew that no matter in what guise he came the man whose face was now pressed against the bars was a friend.

With a swift, graceful movement she rose to her feet, crossed quickly to the window, and sank upon her knees.

"Speak in a whisper," she said; "and speak quickly. You are in great danger!"

That her first thought was of his safety gave Ford a thrill of shame and pleasure.

Until now Miss Dosia Dale had been only the chief feature in a newspaper story; the unknown quantity in a problem. She had meant no more to him than had the initials on her steamer-trunk. Now, through her beauty, through the distress in her eyes, through her warm and generous nature that had disclosed itself with her first words, she became a living, breathing, lovely, and lovable woman. All of the young man's chivalry leaped to the call. He had gone back several centuries. In feeling, he was a knight-errant rescuing beauty in distress from a dungeon cell. To the girl, he was a reckless young person with a dirty face and eyes that gave confidence. But, though a knight-errant, Ford was a modern knight-errant. He wasted no time in explanations or pretty speeches.

"In two minutes," he whispered, "I'll unlock your door. There's a ladder outside your room to the roof. Once we get to the roof the rest's easy. Should anything go wrong, I'll come back by this fire-escape. Wait at the window until you see your door open. Do you understand?"

The girl answered with an eager nod. The color had flown to her cheek. Her eyes flashed in excitement. A sudden doubt assailed Ford.

"You've no time to put on any more clothes," he commanded.

"I haven't got any!" said the girl.

The knight-errant ran up the fire-escape, pulled himself over the edge of the roof, and, crossing it, dropped through the trap to the landing of the kitchen stairs. Here he expended the greater part of the two minutes he had allowed himself in cautiously opening the door into the hall. He accomplished this without a sound, and in one step crossed the hall to the door that held Miss Dale a prisoner.

Slowly he drew back the bolts. Only the spring lock now barred him from her. With thumb and forefinger he turned the key, pushed the door gently open, and ran into the room.

At the same instant from behind him, within six feet of him, he heard the staircase creak. A bomb bursting could not have shaken him more rudely. He swung on his heel and found, blocking the door, the giant bulk of Prothero regarding him over the barrel of his pistol.

"Don't move!" said the Jew.

At the sound of his voice the girl gave a cry of warning, and sprang forward.

"Go back!" commanded Prothero. His voice was low and soft, and apparently calm, but his face showed white with rage.

Ford had recovered from the shock of the surprise. He, also, was in a rage—a rage of mortification and bitter disappointment.

"Don't point that gun at me!" he blustered.

The sound of leaping footsteps and the voice of Pearsall echoed from the floor below.

"Have you got him?" he called.

Prothero made no reply, nor did he lower his pistol. When Pearsall was at his side, without turning his head, he asked in the same steady tone:

"What shall we do with him?"

The face of Pearsall was white, and furious with fear.

"I told you——" he stormed.

"Never mind what you told me," said the Jew. "What shall we do with him? He knows!"

Ford's mind was working swiftly. He had no real fear of personal danger for the girl or himself. The Jew, he argued, was no fool. He would not risk his neck by open murder. And, as he saw it, escape with the girl might still be possible. He had only to conceal from Prothero his knowledge of the line of retreat over the house-tops, explain his rain-soaked condition, and wait a better chance.

To this end he proceeded to lie briskly and smoothly.

"Of course I know," he taunted. He pointed to his dripping garments. "Do you know where I've been? In the street, placing my men. I have this house surrounded. I am going to walk down those stairs with this young lady. If you try to stop me I have only to blow my police-whistle——"

"And I will blow your brains out!" interrupted the Jew. It was a most unsatisfactory climax.

"You have not been in the street," said Prothero. "You are wet because you hung out of your window signalling to your friend. Do you know why he did not answer your second signal? Because he is lying in an area, with a knife in him!"

"You lie!" cried Ford.

"YOU lie," retorted the Jew quietly, "when you say your men surround this house. You are alone. You are NOT in the police service, you are a busybody meddling with men who think as little of killing you as they did of killing your friend. My servant was placed to watch your window, saw your signal, reported to me. And I found your assistant and threw him into an area, with a knife in him!"

Ford felt the story was untrue. Prothero was trying to frighten him. Out of pure bravado no sane man would boast of murder. But—and at the thought Ford felt a touch of real fear—was the man sane? It was a most unpleasant contingency. Between a fight with an angry man and an insane man the difference was appreciable. From this new view-point Ford regarded his adversary with increased wariness; he watched him as he would a mad dog. He regretted extremely he had not brought his revolver.

With his automatic pistol still covering Ford, Prothero spoke to Pearsall.

"I found him," he recited, as though testing the story he would tell later, "prowling through my house at night. Mistaking him for a burglar, I killed him. The kitchen window will be found open, with the lock broken, showing how he gained an entrance. Why not?" he demanded.

"Because," protested Pearsall, in terror, "the man outside will tell——"

Ford shouted in genuine relief.

"Exactly!" he cried. "The man outside, who is not down an area with a knife in him, but who at this moment is bringing the police—he will tell!"

As though he had not been interrupted, Prothero continued thoughtfully:

"What they may say he expected to find here, I can explain away later. The point is that I found a strange man, hatless, dishevelled, prowling in my house. I called on him to halt; he ran, I fired, and unfortunately killed him. An Englishman's home is his castle; an English jury——"

"An English jury," said Ford briskly, "is the last thing you want to meet—— It isn't a Chicago jury."

The Jew flung back his head as though Ford had struck him in the face.

"Ah!" he purred, "you know that, too, do you?" The purr increased to a snarl. "You know too much!"

For Pearsall, his tone seemed to bear an alarming meaning. He sprang toward Prothero, and laid both hands upon his disengaged arm.

"For God's sake," he pleaded, "come away! He can't hurt you—not alive; but dead, he'll hang you—hang us both. We must go, now, this moment." He dragged impotently at the left arm of the giant. "Come!" he begged.

Whether moved by Pearsall's words or by some thought of his own, Prothero nodded in assent. He addressed himself to Ford.

"I don't know what to do with you," he said, "so I will consult with my friend outside this door. While we talk, we will lock you in. We can hear any move you make. If you raise the window or call I will open the door and kill you—you and that woman!"

With a quick gesture, he swung to the door, and the spring lock snapped. An instant later the bolts were noisily driven home.

When the second bolt shot into place, Ford turned and looked at Miss Dale.

"This is a hell of a note!" he said

III

Outside the locked door the voices of the two men rose in fierce whispers. But Ford regarded them not at all. With the swiftness of a squirrel caught in a cage, he darted on tiptoe from side to side searching the confines of his prison. He halted close to Miss Dale and pointed at the windows.

"Have you ever tried to loosen those bars?" he whispered.

The girl nodded and, in pantomime that spoke of failure, shrugged her shoulders.

"What did you see?" demanded Ford hopefully.

The girl destroyed his hope with a shake of her head and a swift smile.

"Scissors," she said; "but they found them and took them away." Ford pointed at the open grate.

"Where's the poker?" he demanded.

"They took that, too. I bent it trying to pry the bars. So they knew."

The man gave her a quick, pleased glance, then turned his eyes to the door that led into the room that looked upon the street.

"Is that door locked?"

"No," the girl told him. "But the door from it into the hall is fastened, like the other, with a spring lock and two bolts."

Ford cautiously opened the door into the room adjoining, and, except for a bed and wash-stand, found it empty. On tiptoe he ran to the windows. Sowell Street was deserted. He returned to Miss Dale, again closing the door between the two rooms.

"The nurse," Miss Dale whispered, "when she is on duty, leaves that door open so that she can watch me; when she goes downstairs, she locks and bolts the door from that room to the hall. It's locked now."

"What's the nurse like?"

The girl gave a shudder that seemed to Ford sufficiently descriptive. Her lips tightened in a hard, straight line.

"She's not human," she said. "I begged her to help me, appealed to her in every way; then I tried a dozen times to get past her to the stairs."

"Well?"

The girl frowned, and with a gesture signified her surroundings.

"I'm still here," she said.

She bent suddenly forward and, with her hand on his shoulder, turned the man so that he faced the cot.

"The mattress on that bed," she whispered, "rests on two iron rods. They are loose and can be lifted. I planned to smash the lock, but the noise would have brought Prothero. But you could defend yourself with one of them."

Ford had already run to the cot and dropped to his knees. He found the mattress supported on strips of iron resting loosely in sockets at the head and foot. He raised the one nearer him, and then, after a moment of hesitation, let it drop into place.

"That's fine!" he whispered. "Good as a crowbar.'" He shook his head in sudden indecision. "But I don't just know how to use it. His automatic could shoot six times before I could swing that thing on him once. And if I have it in my hands when he opens the door, he'll shoot, and he may hit you. But if I leave it where it is, he won't know I know it's there, and it may come in very handy later."

In complete disapproval the girl shook her head. Her eyes filled with concern. "You must not fight him," she ordered. "I mean, not for me. You don't know the danger. The man's not sane. He won't give you a chance. He's mad. You have no right to risk your life for a stranger. I'll not permit it——"

Ford held up his hand for silence. With a jerk of his head he signified the door. "They've stopped talking," he whispered.

Straining to hear, the two leaned forward, but from the hall there came no sound. The girl raised her eyebrows questioningly.

"Have they gone?" she breathed.

"If I knew that," protested Ford, "we wouldn't be here!"

In answer to his doubt a smart rap, as though from the butt of a revolver, fell upon the door. The voice of Prothero spoke sharply:

"You, who call yourself Grant!" he shouted.

Before answering, Ford drew Miss Dale and himself away from the line of the door, and so placed the girl with her back to the wall that if the door opened she would be behind it. "Yes," he answered.

"Pearsall and I," called Prothero, "have decided how to dispose of you—of both of you. He has gone below to make preparations. I am on guard. If you try to break out or call for help, I'll shoot you as I warned you!"

"And I warn you," shouted Ford, "if this lady and I do not instantly leave this house, or if any harm comes to her, you will hang for it!" Prothero laughed jeeringly.

"Who will hang me?" he mocked.

"My friends," retorted Ford. "They know I am in this house. They know WHY I am here. Unless they see Miss Dale and myself walk out of it in safety, they will never let you leave it. Don't be a fool, Prothero!" he shouted. "You know I am telling the truth. You know your only chance for mercy is to open that door and let us go free."

For over a minute Ford waited, but from the hall there was no answer.

After another minute of silence, Ford turned and gazed inquiringly at Miss Dale.

"Prothero!" he called.

Again for a full minute he waited and again called, and then, as there still was no reply, he struck the door sharply with his knuckles. On the instant the voice of the Jew rang forth in an angry bellow.

"Keep away from that door!" he commanded.

Ford turned to Miss Dale and bent his head close to hers.

"Now, why the devil didn't he answer?" he whispered. "Was it because he wasn't there; or is he planning to steal away and wants us to think that even if he does not answer, he's still outside?" The girl nodded eagerly.

"This is it," she whispered. "My uncle is a coward or rather he is very wise, and has left the house. And Prothero means to follow, but he wants us to think he's still on guard. If we only KNEW!" she exclaimed.

As though in answer to her thought, the voice of Prothero called to them.

"Don't speak to me again," he warned. "If you do, I'll not answer, or I'll shoot!"

Flattened against the wall, close to the hinges of the door, Ford replied flippantly and defiantly:

"That makes conversation difficult, doesn't it?" he called.

There was a bursting report, and a bullet splintered the panel of the door, flattened itself against the fireplace, and fell tinkling into the grate.

"I hope I hit you!" roared the Jew.

Ford pressed his lips tightly together. Whatever happy retort may have risen to them was forever lost. For an exchange of repartee, the moment did not seem propitious.

"Perhaps now," jeered Prothero, "you'll believe I'm in earnest!"

Ford still resisted any temptation to reply. He grinned apologetically at the girl and shrugged his shoulders. Her face was white, but it was white from excitement, not from fear.

"What did I tell you?" she whispered. "He IS mad— quite mad!"

Ford glanced at the bullet-hole in the panel of the door. It was on a line with his heart. He looked at Miss Dale; her shoulder was on a level with his own, and her eyes were following his.

"In case he does that again," said Ford, "we would be more comfortable sitting down."

With their shoulders against the wall, the two young people sank to the floor. The position seemed to appeal to them as humorous, and, when their eyes met, they smiled.

"To a spectator," whispered Ford encouragingly, "we MIGHT appear to be getting the worst of this. But, as a matter of fact, every minute Cuthbert does not come means that the next minute may bring him."

"You don't believe he was hurt?" asked the girl.

"No," said Ford. "I believe Prothero found him, and I believe there may have been a fight. But you heard what Pearsall said: 'The man outside will tell.' If Cuthbert's in a position to tell, he is not down an area with a knife in him."

He was interrupted by a faint report from the lowest floor, as though the door to the street had been sharply slammed. Miss Dale showed that she also had heard it.

"My uncle," she said, "making his escape!"

"It may be," Ford answered.

The report did not suggest to him the slamming of a door, but he saw no reason for saying so to the girl.

With his fingers locked across his knees, Ford was leaning forward, his eyes frowning, his lips tightly shut. At his side the girl regarded him covertly. His broad shoulders, almost touching hers, his strong jaw projecting aggressively, and the alert, observant eyes gave her confidence. For three weeks she had been making a fight single-handed. But she was now willing to cease struggling and relax. Quite happily she placed herself and her safety in the keeping of a stranger.

Half to herself, half to the man, she murmured: "It is like 'The Sieur de Maletroit's Door.'"

Without looking at her, Ford shook his head and smiled.

"No such luck," he corrected grimly. "That young man was given a choice. The moment he was willing to marry the girl he could have walked out of the room free. I do not recall Prothero's saying I can escape death by any such charming alternative." The girl interrupted quickly.

"No," she said; "you are not at all like that young man. He stumbled in by chance. You came on purpose to help me. It was fine, unselfish."

"It was not," returned Ford. "My motive was absolutely selfish. It was not to help you I came, but to be able to tell about it later. It is my business to do that. And before I saw you, it was all in the day's work. But after I saw you it was no longer a part of the day's work; it became a matter of a life time."

The girl at his side laughed softly and lightly. "A lifetime is not long," she said, "when you are locked in a room and a madman is shooting at you. It may last only an hour."

"Whether it lasts an hour or many years," said Ford, "it can mean to me now only one thing——" He turned quickly and looked in her face boldly and steadily: "You," he said.

The girl did not avoid his eyes, but returned his glance with one as steady as his own. "You are an amusing person," she said. "Do you feel it is necessary to keep up my courage with pretty speeches?"

"I made no pretty speech," said Ford. "I proclaimed a fact. You are the most charming person that ever came into my life, and whether Prothero shoots us up, or whether we live to get back to God's country, you will never leave it."

The girl pretended to consider his speech critically. "It would be almost a compliment," she said, "if it were intelligent, but when you know nothing of me—it is merely impertinent."

"I know this much of you," returned Ford, calmly; "I know you are fine and generous, for your first speech to me, in spite of your own danger, was for my safety. I know you are brave, for I see you now facing death without dismay."

He was again suddenly halted by, two sharp reports. They came from the room directly below them. It was no longer possible to pretend to misinterpret their significance.

"Prothero!" exclaimed Ford, "and his pistol!"

They waited breathlessly for what might follow: an outcry, the sound of a body falling, a third pistol-shot. But throughout the house there was silence.

"If you really think we are in such danger," declared Miss Dale, "we are wasting time!"

"We are NOT wasting time," protested Ford; "we are really gaining time, for each minute Cuthbert and the police are drawing nearer, and to move about only invites a bullet. And, what is of more importance," he went on quickly, as though to turn her mind from the mysterious pistol-shots, "should we get out of this alive, I shall already have said what under ordinary conditions I might not have found the courage to tell you in many months." He waited as though hopeful of a reply, but Miss Dale remained silent. "They say," continued Ford, "when a man is drowning his whole life passes in review. We are drowning, and yet I find I can see into the past no further than the last half-hour. I find life began only then, when I looked through the bars of that window and found YOU!"

With the palm of her hand the girl struck the floor sharply. "This is neither the time," she exclaimed, "nor the place to——"

"I did not choose the place," Ford pointed out. "It was forced upon me with a gun. But the TIME is excellent. At such a time one speaks only what is true."

"You certainly have a strange sense of humor," she said, "but when you are risking your life to help me, how can I be angry?"

"Of course you can't," Ford agreed heartily; "you could not be so conventional."

"But I AM conventional!" protested Miss Dale. "And I am not USED to having young men tell me they have 'come into my life to stay'—certainly not young men who come into my life by way of a trap-door, and without an introduction, without a name, without even a hat! It's absurd! It's not real! It's a nightmare!"

"The whole situation is absurd!" Ford declared. "Here we are in the heart of London, surrounded by telephones, taxicabs, police—at least, hope we are surrounded by police and yet we are crawling around the floor on our hands and knees dodging bullets. I wish it were a nightmare. But, as it's not"—he rose to his feet—"I think I'll try——"

He was interrupted by a sharp blow upon the door and the voice of Prothero.

"You, navy officer!" he panted. "Come to the door! Stand close to it so that I needn't shout. Come, quick!"

Ford made no answer. Motioning to Miss Dale to remain where she was, he ran noiselessly to the bed, and from beneath the mattress lifted one of the iron bars upon which it rested. Grasping it at one end, he swung the bar swiftly as a man tests the weight of a baseball bat. As a weapon it seemed to satisfy him, for he smiled. Then once more he placed himself with his back to the wall. "Do you hear me?" roared Prothero.

"I hear you!" returned Ford. "If you want to talk to me, open the door and come inside."

"Listen to me," called Prothero. "If I open the door you may act the fool, and I will have to shoot you, and I have made up my mind to let you live. You will soon have this house to yourselves. In a few moments I will leave it, but where I am going I'll need money, and I want the bank-notes in that blue envelope." Ford swung the iron club in short half-circles.

"Come in and get them!" he called.

"Don't trifle with me!" roared the Jew, "I may change my mind. Shove the money through the crack under the door."

"And get shot!" returned Ford. "Not bit like it!"

"If, in one minute," shouted Prothero, "I don't see the money coming through that crack, I'll begin shooting through this door, and neither of you will live!"

Resting the bar in the crook of his elbow, Ford snatched the bank-notes from the envelope, and, sticking them in his pocket, placed the empty envelope on the floor. Still keeping out of range, and using his iron bar as a croupier uses his rake, he pushed the envelope across the carpet and under the door. When half of it had disappeared from the other side of the door, it was snatched from view.

An instant later there was a scream of anger and on a line where Ford would have been, had he knelt to shove the envelope under the door, three bullets splintered through the panel.

At the same moment the girl caught him by the wrist. Unheeding the attack upon the door, her eyes were fixed upon the windows. With her free hand she pointed at the one at which Ford had first appeared. The blind was still raised a few inches, and they saw that the night was lit with a strange and brilliant radiance. The storm had passed, and from all the houses that backed upon the one in which they were prisoners lights blazed from every window, and in each were crowded many people, and upon the roof-tops in silhouette from the glare of the street lamps below, and in the yards and clinging to the walls that separated them, were hundreds of other dark, shadowy groups changing and swaying. And from them rose the confused, inarticulate, terrifying murmur of a mob. It was as though they were on a race-track at night facing a great grandstand peopled with an army of ghosts. With the girl at his side, Ford sprang to the window and threw up the blind, and as they clung to the bars, peering into the night, the light in the room fell full upon them. And in an instant from the windows opposite, from the yards below, and from the house-tops came a savage, exultant yell of welcome, a confusion of cries' orders, entreaties, a great roar of warning. At the sound, Ford could feel the girl at his side tremble.

"What does it mean?" she cried.

"Cuthbert has raised the neighborhood!" shouted Ford jubilantly. "Or else"—he cried in sudden enlightenment—"those shots we heard."

The girl stopped him with a low cry of fear. She thrust her arms between the bars and pointed. In the yard below them was the sloping roof of the kitchen. It stretched from the house to the wall of the back yard. Above the wall from the yard beyond rose a ladder, and, face down upon the roof, awry and sprawling, were the motionless forms of two men. Their shining capes and heavy helmets proclaimed their calling.

"The police!" exclaimed Ford. "And the shots we thought were for those in the house were for THEM! This is what has happened," he whispered eagerly: "Prothero attacked Cuthbert. Cuthbert gets away and goes to the police. He tells them you are here a prisoner, that I am here probably a prisoner, and of the attack upon himself. The police try to make an entrance from the street—that was the first shot we heard—and are driven back; then they try to creep in from the yard, and those poor devils were killed."

As he spoke a sudden silence had fallen, a silence as startling as had been the shout of warning. Some fresh attack upon the house which the prisoners could not see, but which must be visible to those in the houses opposite was going forward.

"Perhaps they are on the roof,'" whispered Ford joyfully. "They'll be through the trap in a minute, and you'll be free!"

"No!" said the girl.

She also spoke in a whisper, as though she feared Prothero might hear her. And with her hand she again pointed. Cautiously above the top of the ladder appeared the head and shoulders of a man. He wore a policeman's helmet, but, warned by the fate of his comrades, he came armed. Balancing himself with his left hand on the rung of the ladder, he raised the other and pointed a revolver. It was apparently at the two prisoners, and Miss Dale sprang to one side.

"Standstill!" commanded Ford. "He knows who YOU are! You heard that yell when they saw you? They know you are the prisoner, and they are glad you're still alive. That officer is aiming at the window BELOW us. He's after the men who murdered his mates."

From the window directly beneath them came the crash of a rifle, and from the top of the ladder the revolver of the police officer blazed in the darkness. Again the rifle crashed, and the man on the ladder jerked his hands above his head and pitched backward. Ford looked into the face of the girl and found her eyes filled with horror.

"Where is my uncle, Pearsall?" she faltered. "He has two rifles—for shooting in Scotland. Was that a rifle that——" Her lips refused to finish the question.

"It was a rifle," Ford stammered, "but probably Prothero——"

Even as he spoke the voice of the Jew rose in a shriek from the floor below them, but not from the window below them. The sound was from the front room opening on Sowell Street. In the awed silence that had suddenly fallen his shrieks carried sharply. They were more like the snarls and ravings of an animal than the outcries of a man.

"Take THAT!" he shouted, with a flood of oaths, "and THAT, and THAT!"

Each word was punctuated by the report of his automatic, and to the amazement of Ford, was instantly answered from Sowell Street by a scattered volley of rifle and pistol shots.

"This isn't a fight," he cried, "it's a battle!"

With Miss Dale at his side, he ran into the front room, and, raising the blind, appeared at the window. And instantly, as at the other end of the house, there was, at sight of the woman's figure, a tumult of cries, a shout of warning, and a great roar of welcome. From beneath them a man ran into the deserted street, and in the glare of the gas-lamp Ford saw his white, upturned face. He was without a hat and his head was circled by a bandage. But Ford recognized Cuthbert.

"That's Ford!" he cried, pointing. "And the girl's with him!" He turned to a group of men crouching in the doorway of the next house to the one in which Ford was imprisoned. "The girl's alive!" he shouted.

"The girl's alive!" The words were caught up and flung from window to window, from house-top to house-top, with savage, jubilant cheers. Ford pushed Miss Dale forward.

"Let them see you," he said, "and you will never see a stranger sight."

Below them, Sowell Street, glistening with rain and snow, lay empty, but at either end of it, held back by an army of police, were black masses of men, and beyond them more men packed upon the tops of taxicabs and hansoms, stretching as far as the street-lamps showed, and on the roofs shadowy forms crept cautiously from chimney to chimney; and in the windows of darkened rooms opposite, from behind barricades of mattresses and upturned tables, rifles appeared stealthily, to be lost in a sudden flash of flame. And with these flashes were others that came from windows and roofs with the report of a bursting bomb, and that, on the instant, turned night into day, and then left the darkness more dark.

Ford gave a cry of delight.

"They're taking flash-light photographs," he cried jubilantly. "Well done, you Pressmen!" The instinct of the reporter became compelling. "If they're alive to develop those photographs to-night," he exclaimed eagerly, "Cuthbert will send them by special messenger, in time to catch the MAURETANIA and the REPUBLIC will have them by Sunday. I mayn't be alive to see them," he added regretfully, "but what a feature for the Sunday supplement!"

As the eyes of the two prisoners became accustomed to the darkness, they saw that the street was not, as at first they had supposed, entirely empty. Directly below them in the gutter, where to approach it was to invite instant death from Prothero's pistol, lay the dead body of a policeman, and at the nearer end of the street, not fifty yards from them, were three other prostrate forms. But these forms were animate, and alive to good purpose. From a public-house on the corner a row of yellow lamps showed them clearly. Stretched on pieces of board, and mats commandeered from hallways and cabs, each of the three men lay at full length, nursing a rifle. Their belted gray overcoats, flat, visored caps, and the set of their shoulders marked them for soldiers.

"For the love of Heaven!" exclaimed Ford incredulously, "they've called out the Guards!"

As unconcernedly as though facing the butts at a rifle-range, the three sharp-shooters were firing point-blank at the windows from which Prothero and Pearsall were waging their war to the death upon the instruments of law and order. Beside them, on his knees in the snow, a young man with the silver hilt of an officer's sword showing through the slit in his greatcoat, was giving commands; and at the other end of the street, a brother officer in evening dress was directing other sharp-shooters, bending over them like the coach of a tug-of-war team, pointing with white-gloved fingers. On the side of the street from which Prothero was firing, huddled in a doorway, were a group of officials, inspectors of police, fire chiefs in brass helmets, more officers of the Guards in bear-skins, and, wrapped in a fur coat, the youthful Horne Secretary. Ford saw him wave his arm, and at his bidding the cordon of police broke, and slowly forcing its way through the mass of people came a huge touring-car, its two blazing eyes sending before it great shafts of light. The driver of the car wasted no time in taking up his position. Dashing half-way down the street, he as swiftly backed the automobile over the gutter and up on the sidewalk, so that the lights in front fell full on the door of No. 40. Then, covered by the fire from the roofs, he sprang to the lamps and tilted them until they threw their shafts into the windows of the third story. Prothero's hiding-place was now as clearly exposed as though it were held in the circle of a spot-light, and at the success of the maneuver the great mob raised an applauding cheer. But the triumph was brief. In a minute the blazing lamps had been shattered by bullets, and once more, save for the fierce flashes from rifles and pistols, Sowell Street lay in darkness.

Ford drew Miss Dale back into the room.

"Those men below," he said, "are mad. Prothero's always been mad, and your Pearsall is mad with drugs. And the sight of blood has made them maniacs. They know they now have no chance to live. There's no fear or hope to hold them, and one life more or less means nothing. If they should return here——"

He hesitated, but the girl nodded quickly. "I understand," she said.

"I'm going to try to break down the door and get to the roof," explained Ford. "My hope is that this attack will keep them from hearing, and——"

"No," protested the girl. "They will hear you, and they will kill you."

"They may take it into their crazy heads to do that, anyway," protested Ford, "so the sooner I get you away, the better. I've only to smash the panels close to the bolts, put my arm through the hole, and draw the bolts back. Then, another blow on the spring lock when the firing is loudest, and we are in the hall. Should anything happen to me, you must know how to make your escape alone. Across the hall is a door leading to an iron ladder. That ladder leads to a trap-door. The trap-door is open. When you reach the roof, run westward toward a lighted building."

"I am not going without you," said Miss Dale quietly; "not after what you have done for me."

76

"I haven't done anything for you yet," objected Ford. "But in case I get caught I mean to make sure there will be others on hand who will."

He pulled his pencil and a letter from his pocket, and on the back of the envelope wrote rapidly: "I will try to get Miss Dale up through the trap in the roof. You can reach the roof by means of the apartment house in Devonshire Street. Send men to meet her."

In the groups of officials half hidden in the doorway farther down the street, he could make out the bandaged head of Cuthbert. "Cuthbert!" he called. Weighting the envelope with a coin, he threw it into the air. It fell in the gutter, under a lamp-post, and full in view, and at once the two madmen below splashed the street around it with bullets. But, indifferent to the bullets, a policeman sprang from a dark areaway and flung himself upon it. The next moment he staggered. Then limping, but holding himself erect, he ran heavily toward the group of officials. The Home Secretary snatched the envelope from him, and held it toward the light.

In his desire to learn if his message had reached those on the outside, Ford leaned far over the sill of the window. His imprudence was all but fatal. From the roof opposite there came a sudden yell of warning, from directly below him a flash, and a bullet grazed his forehead and shattered the window-pane above him. He was deluged with a shower of broken glass. Stunned and bleeding, he sprang back.

With a cry of concern, Miss Dale ran toward him.

"It's nothing!" stammered Ford. "It only means I must waste no more time." He balanced his iron rod as he would a pikestaff, and aimed it at the upper half of the door to the hall.

"When the next volley comes," he said, "I'll smash the panel."

With the bar raised high, his muscles on a strain, he stood alert and poised, waiting for a shot from the room below to call forth an answering volley from the house-tops. But no sound came from below. And the sharp-shooters, waiting for the madmen to expose themselves, held their fire.

Ford's muscles relaxed, and he lowered his weapon. He turned his eyes inquiringly to the girl. "What's THIS mean?" he demanded. Unconsciously his voice had again dropped to a whisper.

"They're short of ammunition," said the girl, in a tone as low as his own; "or they are coming HERE."

With a peremptory gesture, Ford waved her toward the room adjoining and then ran to the window.

The girl was leaning forward with her face close to the door. She held the finger of one hand to her lips. With the other hand she beckoned. Ford ran to her side.

"Some one is moving in the hall," she whispered. "Perhaps they are escaping by the roof? No," she corrected herself. "They seem to be running down the stairs again. Now they are coming back. Do you hear?" she asked. "It sounds like some one running up and down the stairs. What can it mean?"

From the direction of the staircase Ford heard a curious creaking sound as of many light footsteps. He gave a cry of relief.

"The police!" he shouted jubilantly. "They've entered through the roof, and they're going to attack in the rear. You're SAFE!" he cried.

He sprang away from the door and, with two swinging blows, smashed the broad panel. And then, with a cry, he staggered backward. Full in his face, through the break he had made, swept a hot wave of burning cinders. Through the broken panel he saw the hall choked with smoke, the steps of the staircase and the stair-rails wrapped in flame.

"The house is on fire!" he cried. "They've taken to the roof and set fire to the stairs behind them!" With the full strength of his arms and shoulders he struck and smashed the iron bar against the door. But the bolts held, and through each fresh opening he made in the panels the burning cinders, drawn by the draft from the windows, swept into the room. From the street a mighty yell of consternation told them the fire had been discovered. Miss Dale ran to the window, and the yell turned to a great cry of warning. The air was rent with frantic voices. "Jump!" cried some. "Go back!" entreated others. The fire chief ran into the street directly below her and shouted at her through his hands. "Wait for the life-net!" he commanded. "Wait for the ladders!"

"Ladders!" panted Ford. "Before they can get their engines through that mob——"

Through the jagged opening in the door he thrust his arm and jerked free the upper bolt. An instant later he had kicked the lower panel into splinters and withdrawn the second bolt, and at last, under the savage onslaught of his iron bar, the spring lock flew apart. The hall lay open before him. On one side of it the burning staircase was a well of flame; at his feet, the matting on the floor was burning fiercely. He raced into the bedroom and returned instantly, carrying a blanket and a towel dripping with water. He pressed the towel across the girl's mouth and nostrils. "Hold it there!" he commanded. Blinded by the bandage, Miss Dale could see nothing, but she felt herself suddenly wrapped in the blanket and then lifted high in Ford's arms. She gave a cry of protest, but the next instant he was running with her swiftly while the flames from the stair-well scorched her hair. She was suddenly tumbled to her feet, the towel and blanket snatched away, and she saw Ford hanging from an iron ladder holding out his hand. She clasped it, and he drew her after him, the flames and cinders pursuing and snatching hungrily.

But an instant later the cold night air smote her in the face, from hundreds of hoarse throats a yell of welcome greeted her, and she found herself on the roof, dazed and breathless, and free.

At the same moment the lifting fire-ladder reached the sill of the third-story window, and a fireman, shielding his face from the flames, peered into the blazing room. What he saw showed him there were no lives to rescue. Stretched on the floor, with their clothing in cinders and the flames licking at the flesh, were the bodies of the two murderers.

A bullet-hole in the forehead of each showed that self-destruction and cremation had seemed a better choice than the gallows and a grave of quick-lime.

On the roof above, two young people stood breathing heavily and happily, staring incredulously into each other's eyes. Running toward them across the roofs, stumbling and falling, were many blue-coated, helmeted angels of peace and law and order.

"How can I tell you?" whispered the girl quickly. "How can I ever thank you? And I was angry," she exclaimed, with self-reproach. "I did not understand you." She gave a little sigh of content. "Now I think I do."

He took her hand, and she did not seem to know that he held it.

"And," she cried, in wonder, "I DON'T EVEN KNOW YOUR NAME!"

The young man seemed to have lost his confidence. For a moment he was silent. "The name's all right!" he said finally. His voice was still a little shaken, a little tremulous. "I only hope you'll like it. It's got to last you a long time!"